Boris the Boastful Frog

Karen Hodgson and Steve Cox

In a pond at the bottom of a muddy field, there lived a frog called Boris. He was big and strong and handsome, but he was also boastful.

When the other frogs smiled at him, Boris would smile back, but then say,
"My smile is wider than yours. I have the widest smile in this pond."

When the other frogs croaked, "Hello!",
he would croak, "**Hello!**" back, but then add,
"My croaking is louder than yours. I have the loudest
croak in this pond."

When the frogs invited him to join in their games, he
would spoil the fun by boasting that he could ...

... jump higher ...

... dive deeper ...

... or swim faster ...

... than anyone else. And he could.

Soon, the other frogs stopped being friendly, and Boris was left to sit on a lily pad alone and admire his reflection.

One afternoon, while Boris sat soaking up the sun, a grasshopper flitted by.

"What kind of a skinny fellow are you?" croaked Boris.

"I'm a grasshopper," said the grasshopper.

"Oh really?" said the frog. "What do grasshoppers do?"

"Hop," replied the grasshopper and he ...

... hopped ...

... onto a nearby bulrush.

The frog laughed. "That's not hopping," he croaked. "If you want to see real hopping, watch this!"

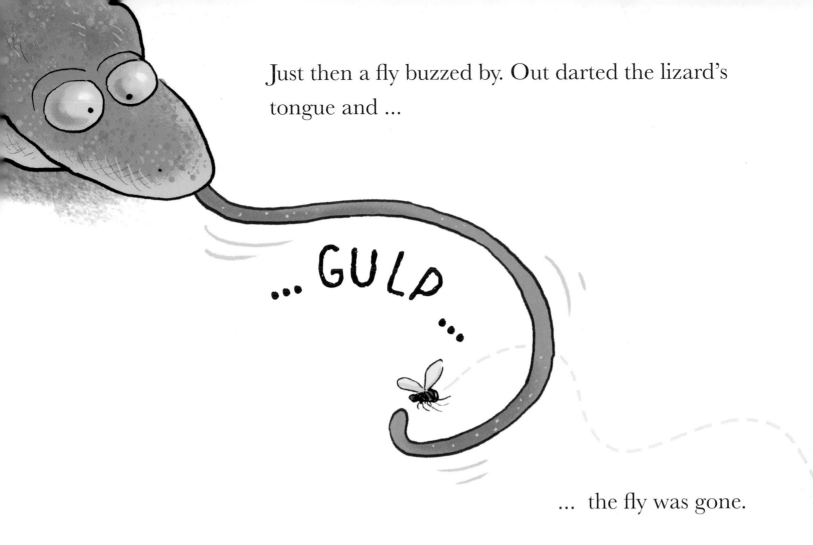

Just then a fly buzzed by. Out darted the lizard's tongue and ...

... GULP ...

... the fly was gone.

Boris laughed. "Call that catching flies?" he croaked. "If you want to see real fly-catching, watch this!"

He flicked out his long tongue,

curled it around three gnats and ...

... Gulululup ...

... swallowed them in one go.

The lizard shook his head sadly and went on his way.

Before long, a third visitor arrived at the pond; a pretty little bird with a bright blue stripe along his back.

"Hello," he chirped as he landed on the branch of a nearby tree.

"What kind of a feathery fellow are you?" said Boris.

"I'm a kingfisher," replied the bird.

"A **king** indeed," scoffed the frog.

"What does a kingfisher do?"

"Fish," said the bird. Then quick as a flash, he darted down into the water and returned with a small minnow in his beak.

Boris laughed. "That's not fishing," he croaked. "If you want to see real fishing, watch this!"

... Splooooosshhhh ...

Once again, Boris bent his powerful legs and this time dived to the bottom of the pond. He returned with a whole mouthful of minnows.

The kingfisher shook his head sadly and flew on his way.

The day had begun to cool when yet another stranger called at the pond. It was the ugliest creature Boris had ever seen.

"What kind of a warty fellow are you?" he croaked.

"A toad," said the toad.

"And what do toads do?" asked Boris.

The toad thought for a moment. "We do the same as frogs mostly," he said.

Then he added, "Oh, and we do this…"

He took a deep breath and puffed himself up until he was as fat and round as a football.

Boris frowned. He'd never tried that. All the same, he wasn't going to be beaten by an ugly, old toad.

"That's nothing!" he said. "Watch this!"

The frog took a deep breath, then closed his mouth and blew.

He blew so hard that his eyes bulged and his shiny green skin turned pink ...

... but he couldn't make himself half as big as the toad.

The toad looked worried. "Frogs can't do that," he said.

"I can!" boasted Boris. "Watch again!"

This time Boris took a deeper breath and blew with all his might. He turned **pink**, and then **red**, but it was useless, he still couldn't make himself as big as the toad.

"You're wasting your time," said the toad.

Boris took a still deeper breath, closed his mouth and blew.
He blew and blew until he turned ...

... pink, and then red, and then deep, deep purple ...

... and then ...

Boris was no more.

The toad shook his head sadly and went on his way.

The End

Published by
Hogs Back Books
The Stables
Down Place
Hogs Back
Guildford GU3 1DE
www.hogsbackbooks.com

Printed in Singapore
ISBN: 978-1-907432-10-1
British Library Cataloguing-in-Publication Data.
A catalogue record for this book is available from the British Library.
1 3 5 4 2